A Katie Dog Day
on
Nantucket

by Karen G. Parvey
illustrated by Anabeth Guthrie

Dedicated to Ben because every dog needs a boy

ISLAND DOG • MEMPHIS

Copyright © 1996 All rights reserved including the right to
reproduction in whole or in part in any form.
Library of Congress Card Catalogue Number: 95-94818.
ISBN: 0964868555
Printed in the United States of America
by Worzalla Publishing Co., Wisconsin

KATIE'S BONE

KATIE'S WHALE

KATIE'S BALL

BONE APPÉTIT
KATIE'S BOWL

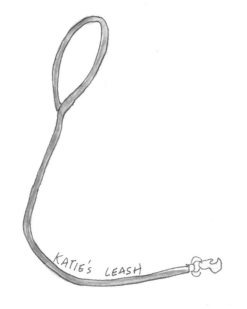

KATIE'S BLANKET

My name is Katie and I am the luckiest dog,
because I summer on an island of fog.
That island is NANTUCKET. It is 30 miles out
at sea. It is where I love to be.

KATIE'S WHALE

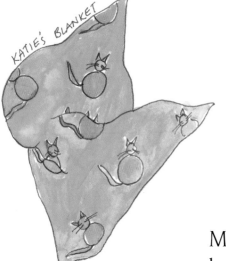

KATIE'S LEASH

KATIE'S BOWL
BONE APPÉTIT

KATIE'S BONE

KATIE'S BANDANA

i gree

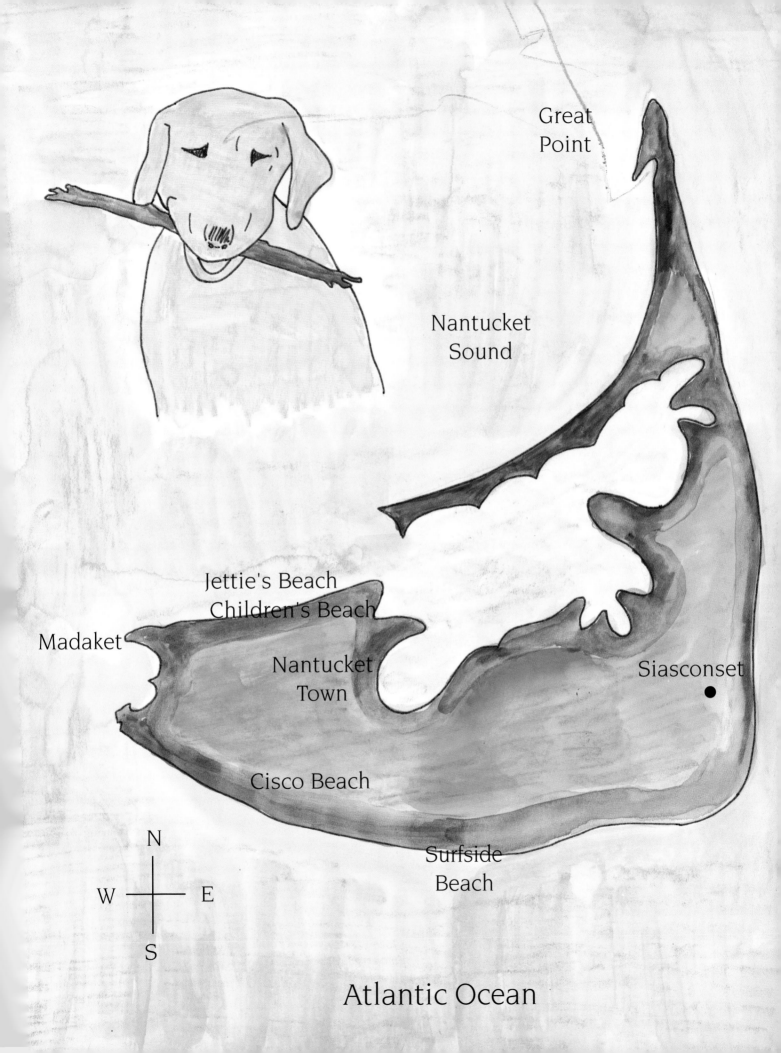

Great
Point

Nantucket
Sound

Jettie's Beach
Children's Beach

Madaket

Nantucket
Town

Siasconset

Cisco Beach

Surfside
Beach

N
W E
S

Atlantic Ocean

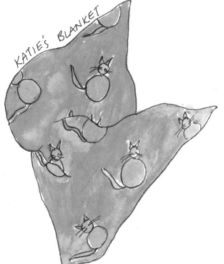

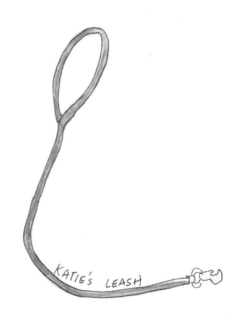

My days are filled with lots of fun
from early morn till setting sun.
There is so much to do.
I will tell it all to you.

KATIE'S WHALE

KATIE'S BONE

KATIE'S BALL

KATIE'S LEASH

BONE APPÉTIT
KATIE'S BOWL

My bowl of food is a welcome sight
after a long sleepy night.
I eat my food and have a drink
as quick as a wink.

KATIE'S BONE

KATIE'S BANDANA

igree

KATIE'S BALL

BONE APPÉTIT
KATIE'S BOWL

KATIE'S BLANKET

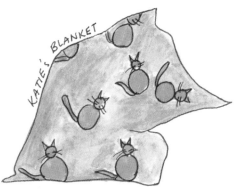

KATIE'S WHALE

KATIE'S WHALE

KATIE'S BONE

KATIE'S BALL

KATIE'S LEASH

BONE APPÉTIT
KATIE'S BOWL

KATIE'S BONE

I get my leash from the hook.
Come on downtown to shop and look.

KATIE'S BANDANA

i gree

KATIE'S BALL

BONE APPÉTIT
KATIE'S BOWL

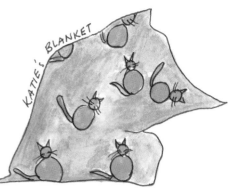

KATIE'S BLANKET

KATIE'S WHALE

KATIE'S BONE

KATIE'S WHALE

KATIE'S BALL

BONE APPÉTIT

KATIE'S BOWL

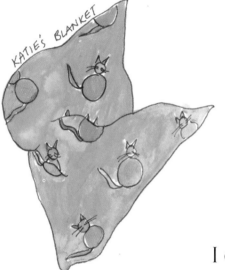

KATIE'S BLANKET

I carry my leash in my mouth
as we walk to town heading south.

KATIE'S WHALE

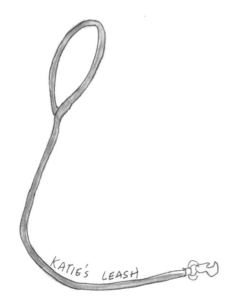

KATIE'S LEASH

KATIE'S BOWL

BONE APPÉTIT

KATIE'S BONE

KATIE'S BANDANA

i gree

KATIE'S WHALE

KATIE'S BONE

KATIE'S BALL

KATIE'S LEASH

BONE APPÉTIT
KATIE'S BOWL

First stop is the bank. I think it is funny....
A bank is where people get money...
but...I get a dog treat
which is really really neat.

KATIE'S BONE

KATIE'S BANDANA

i gree

KATIE'S BALL

BONE APPÉTIT
KATIE'S BOWL

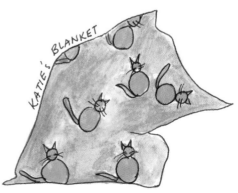

KATIE'S BLANKET

KATIE'S WHALE

KATIE'S WHALE

KATIE'S BONE

KATIE'S BALL

KATIE'S LEASH

BONE APPÉTIT
KATIE'S BOWL

KATIE'S BONE

We wander down Main Street,
where there are many people to greet
on the cobblestone street.
They make such a fuss over me.
Nantucket is the place to be.

KATIE'S BANDANA

i gree

KATIE'S BALL

BONE APPÉTIT
KATIE'S BOWL

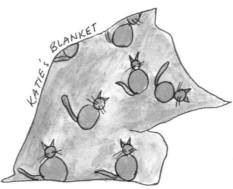

KATIE'S BLANKET

KATIE'S WHALE

KATIE'S BONE

KATIE'S WHALE

KATIE'S BALL

BONE APPÉTIT
KATIE'S BOWL

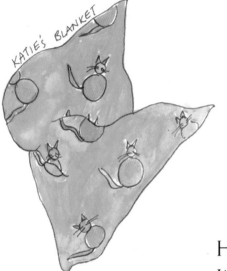
KATIE'S BLANKET

Home we must go and not be slow.
It is noon and time for the beach is soon.

KATIE'S WHALE

KATIE'S LEASH

KATIE'S BOWL
BONE APPÉTIT

KATIE'S BONE

KATIE'S BANDANA
i gree

Towels and chairs are put in the car.
The beach is not very far.
I jump in the car for the short ride.
When we get there it is high tide.

KATIE'S BONE

KATIE'S WHALE

KATIE'S BALL

BONE APPÉTIT
KATIE'S BOWL

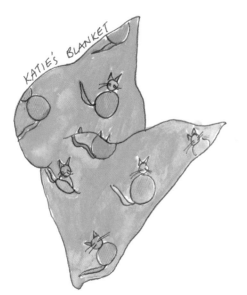

KATIE'S BLANKET

I do so love to swim....
It keeps me so fit and trim.
Things at the beach are never dull.
I always enjoy chasing a gull.

KATIE'S WHALE

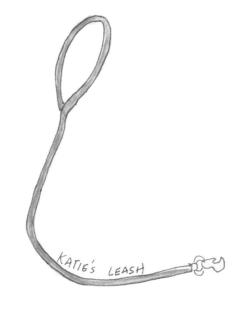

KATIE'S LEASH

KATIE'S BOWL
BONE APPÉTIT

KATIE'S BONE

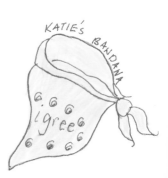

KATIE'S BANDANA
i.gree

KATIE'S BONE

KATIE'S WHALE

KATIE'S BALL

BONE APPÉTIT
KATIE'S BOWL

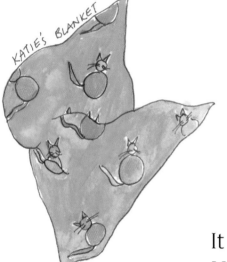

KATIE'S BLANKET

It is getting late. Supper can not wait.
Hurry up. I need an extra cup.

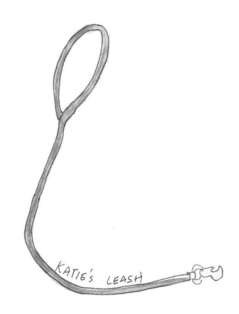

KATIE'S WHALE

KATIE'S LEASH

KATIE'S BOWL
BONE APPÉTIT

KATIE'S BONE

KATIE'S BANDANA
igree

After we dine things are fine.
To Children's Beach we do walk.
It's about seven o'clock.
Many children see me come.
They all want to throw the ball to me.
It is such fun for all to see.

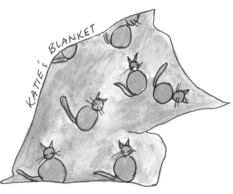

It is getting late and home we must head.
I have had a long day and am ready for bed.
We see a million stars and a moon so bright.
It is a beautiful NANTUCKET night.
Today there was no fog.
I am a very happy dog.

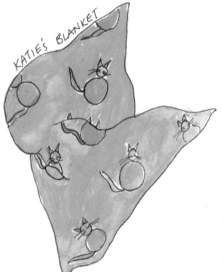

Tomorrow is another island day
and Katie Dog will again be ready to play.
BUT NOW.... I am DOG TIRED......
Let's put out the light.

GOOD NIGHT

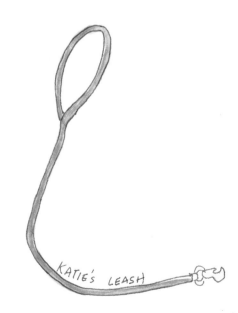

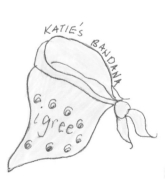

Karen Gilman Parvey was born in Massachusettes and attended Boston University. She received a B.A. and an M.S. in counseling from the University of Memphis. She is a college admissions counselor in Memphis and spends her summers with her family and Katie on Nantucket.

Annabeth Guthrie was born in Memphis, TN and is presently a junior at Mary Washington College in VA. She is majoring in Studio Art and Art History. She has spent the summer on Nantucket where she designed and sold jewelry.